Kittie's Sister Josephine

Elizabeth Jordan

first published in 1906

Kittie James told me this story about her sister Josephine, and when she saw my eye light up the way the true artist's does when he hears a good plot, she said I might use it, if I liked, the next time I "practised literature."

I don't think that was a very nice way to say it, especially when one remembers that Sister Irmingarde read three of my stories to the class in four months; and as I only write one every week, you can see yourself what a good average that was. But it takes noble souls to be humble in the presence of the gifted, and enthusiastic over their success, so only two of my classmates seemed really happy when Sister Irmingarde read my third story aloud. It is hardly necessary to mention the names of these beautiful natures, already so well known to my readers, but I will do it. They were Maudie Joyce and Mabel Blossom, and they are my dearest friends at St. Catharine's. And some day, when I am a real writer and the name of May Iverson shines in gold letters on the tablets of fame, I'll write a book and dedicate it to them. Then, indeed, they will be glad they knew me in my schoolgirl days, and recognized real merit when they saw it, and did not mind the queer things my artistic temperament often makes me do. Oh, what a slave is one to this artistic, emotional nature, and how unhappy, how misunderstood! I don't mean that I am unhappy all the time, of course, but I have Moods. And when I have them life seems so hollow, so empty, so terrible! At such times natures that do not understand me are apt to make mistakes, the way Sister Irmingarde did when she thought I had nervous dyspepsia and made me walk three miles every day, when it was just Soul that was the matter with me. Still, I must admit the exercise helped me. It is so soothing, so restful, so calming to walk on dear nature's breast. Maudie Joyce and Mabel Blossom always know the minute an attack of artistic temperament begins in me. Then they go away quietly and reverently, and I write a story and feel better.

So this time I am going to tell about Kittie James's sister Josephine. In the very beginning I must explain that

Josephine James used to be a pupil at St. Catharine's herself, ages and ages ago, and finally she graduated and left, and began to go into society and look around and decide what her life-work should be. That was long, long before our time—as much as ten years, I should think, and poor Josephine must be twenty-eight or twenty-nine years old now. But Kittie says she is just as nice as she can be, and not a bit poky, and so active and interested in life you'd think she was young. Of course I know such things can be, for my own sister Grace, Mrs. George E. Verbeck, is perfectly lovely and the most popular woman in the society of our city.

But Grace is married, and perhaps that makes a difference. It is said that love keeps the spirit young. However, perhaps I'd better go on about Josephine and not dwell on that. Experienced as we girls are, and drinking of life in deep draughts though we do, we still admit—Maudie, Mabel, and I—that we do not yet know much about love. But one cannot know everything at fifteen, and, as Mabel Blossom always says, “there is yet time.” We all know just the kind of men they’re going to be, though. Mine will be a brave young officer, of course, for a general’s daughter should not marry out of the army, and he will die for his country, leaving me with a broken heart. Maudie Joyce says hers must be a man who will rule her with a rod of iron and break her will and win her respect, and then be gentle and loving and tender. And Mabel Blossom says she's perfectly sure hers will be fat and have a blond mustache and laugh a great deal. Once she said maybe none of us would ever get any; but the look Maudie Joyce and I turned upon her checked her thoughtless words. Life is bitter enough as it is without thinking of dreadful things in the future. I sometimes fear that underneath her girlish gayety Mabel Blossom conceals a morbid nature. But I am forgetting Josephine James. This story will tell why, with all her advantages of wealth and education and beauty, she remained a maiden lady till she was twenty-eight; and she might have kept on, too, if Kittie had not taken matters in hand and settled them for her.

Kittie says Josephine was always romantic and spent long hours of her young life in girlish reveries and dreams. Of course that isn't the way Kittie said it, but if I should tell this story in her crude, unformed fashion, you wouldn't read very far. What Kittie really said was that Josephine used to "moon around the grounds a lot and bawl, and even try to write poetry." I understand Josephine's nature, so I will go on and tell this story in my own way, but you must remember that some of the credit belongs to Kittie and Mabel Blossom; and if Sister Irmingarde reads it in class, they can stand right up with me when the author is called for.

Well, when Josephine James graduated she got a lot of prizes and things, for she was a clever girl, and had not spent all her time writing poetry and thinking deep thoughts about life. She realized the priceless advantages of a broad and thorough education and of association with the most cultivated minds. That sentence comes out of our prospectus. Then she went home and went out a good deal, and was very popular and stopped writing poetry, and her dear parents began to feel happy and hopeful about her, and think she would marry and have a nice family, which is indeed woman's highest, noblest mission in life. But Josephine cherished an ideal.

A great many young men came to see her, and Kittie liked one of them very much indeed—better than all the others. He was handsome, and he laughed and joked a good deal, and always brought Kittie big boxes of candy and called her his little sister. He said she was going to be that in the end, anyhow, and there was no use waiting to give her the title that his heart dictated. He said it just that way. When he took Josephine out in his automobile he'd say, "Let's take the kid, too," and they would, and it did not take Kittie long to understand how things were between George Morgan—for that was indeed his name—and her sister. Little do grown-up people realize how intelligent are the minds of the young, and how keen and penetrating their youthful gaze! Clearly do I recall some things that happened at home, and it would startle papa and mamma to know I know them, but I will not reveal them here. Once I would have done so, in the beginning of my art; but now I have learned to finish one story before I begin another.

Little did Mr. Morgan and Josephine wot that every time she refused him Kittie's young heart burned beneath its sense of wrong, for she did refuse him almost every time they went out together, and yet she kept right on going. You would think she wouldn't, but women's natures are indeed inscrutable. Some authors would stop here and tell what was in Josephine's heart, but this is not that kind of a story. Kittie was only twelve then, and they used big words and talked in a queer way they thought she would not understand; but she did, every time, and she never missed a single word they said. Of course she wasn't listening exactly, you see, because they knew she was there. That makes it different and quite proper. For if Kittie was more intelligent than her elders it was not the poor child's fault.

Things went on like that and got worse and worse, and they had been going on that way for five years. One day Kittie was playing tennis with George at the Country Club, and he had been very kind to her, and all of a sudden Kittie told him she knew all, and how sorry she was for him, and that if he would wait till she grew up she would marry him herself. The poor child was so young, you see, that she did not know how unmaidenly this was. And of course at St. Catharine's when they taught us how to enter and leave rooms and how to act in society and at the table, they didn't think to tell us not to ask young men to marry us. I can add with confidence that Kittie James was the only girl who ever did. I asked the rest afterwards, and they were deeply shocked at the idea.

Well, anyhow, Kittie did it, and she said

George was just as nice as he could be. He told her he had "never listened to a more alluring proposition" (she remembered just the words he used), and that she was "a little trump"; and then he said he feared, alas! it was impossible, as even his strong manhood could not face the prospect of the long and dragging years that lay between. Besides, he said, his heart was already given, and he guessed he'd better stick to Josephine, and would his little sister help him to get her? Kittie wiped her eyes and said she would. She had been crying. It must indeed be a bitter experience to have one's young heart spurned! But George took her into the club-house and gave her tea and lots of English muffins and jam, and somehow Kittie cheered up, for she couldn't help feeling there were still some things in life that were nice.

Of course after that she wanted dreadfully to help George, but there didn't seem to be much she could do. Besides, she had to go right back to school in September, and being a studious child, I need hardly add that her entire mind was then given to her studies. When she went home for the Christmas holidays she took Mabel Blossom with her. Mabel was more than a year older, but Kittie looked up to her, as it is well the young should do to us older girls. Besides, Kittie had had her thirteenth birthday in November, and she was letting down her skirts a little and beginning to think of putting up her hair. She said when she remembered that she asked George to wait till she grew up it made her blush, so you see she was developing very fast.

As I said before, she took Mabel Blossom home for Christmas, and Mr. and Mrs. James were lovely to her, and she had a beautiful time. But Josephine was the best of all. She was just fine. Mabel told me with her own lips that if she hadn't seen Josephine

James's name on the catalogue as a graduate in '93, she never would have believed she was so old. Josephine took the two girls to matinées and gave a little tea for them, and George Morgan was as nice as she was. He was always bringing them candy and violets, exactly as if they were young ladies, and he treated them both with the greatest respect, and stopped calling them the kids when he found they didn't like it. Mabel got as fond of him as Kittie was, and they were both wild to help him to get Josephine to marry him; but she wouldn't, though Kittie finally talked to her long and seriously. I asked Kittie what Josephine said when she did that, and she confessed that Josephine had laughed so she couldn't say anything. That hurt the sensitive child, of course, but grown-ups are all too frequently thoughtless of such things. Had Josephine but listened to Kittie's words on that occasion, it would have saved Kittie a lot of trouble.

Now I am getting to the exciting part of the story. I am always so glad when I get to that. I asked Sister Irmingarde why one couldn't just make the story out of the exciting part, and she took a good deal of time to explain why, but she did not convince me; for besides having the artistic temperament I am strangely logical for one so young. Some day I shall write a story that is all climax from beginning to end. That will show her! But at present I must write according to the severe and cramping rules which she and literature have laid down.

One night Mrs. James gave a large party for Josephine, and of course Mabel and Kittie, being thirteen and fourteen, had to go to bed. It is such things as this that embitter the lives of schoolgirls. But they were allowed to go down and see all the lights and flowers and decorations before people began to come, and they went into the conservatory because that was fixed up with little nooks and things. They got away in and off in a kind of wing of it, and they talked and pretended they were débutantes at the ball, so they stayed longer than they knew. Then they heard voices, and they looked and saw Josephine and Mr. Morgan sitting by the fountain. Before they could move or say they were there, they heard him say this—Kittie remembers just what it was:

"I have spent six years following you, and you've treated me as if I were a dog at the end of a string. This thing must end. I must have you, or I must learn to live without you, and I must know now which it is to be. Josephine, you must give me my final answer to-night."

Wasn't it embarrassing for Kittie and Mabel? They did not want to listen, but some instinct told them

Josephine and George might not be glad to see them then, so they crept behind a lot of tall palms, and Mabel put her fingers in her ears so she wouldn't hear. Kittie didn't. She explained to me afterwards that she thought it being her sister made things kind of different. It was all in the family, anyhow. So Kittie heard Josephine tell Mr. Morgan that the reason she did not marry him was because he was an idler and without an ambition or a purpose in life. And she said she must respect the man she married as well as love him. Then George jumped up quickly and asked if she loved him, and she cried and said she did, but that she would never, never marry him until he did something to win her admiration and prove he was a man. You can imagine how exciting it was for Kittie to see with her own innocent eyes how grown-up people manage such things. She said she was so afraid she'd miss something that she opened them so wide they hurt her afterwards. But she didn't miss anything. She saw him kiss Josephine, too, and then Josephine got up, and he argued and tried to make her change her mind, and she wouldn't, and finally they left the conservatory. After that Kittie and Mabel crept out and rushed up-stairs.

The next morning

Kittie turned to Mabel with a look on her face which Mabel had never seen there before. It was grim and determined. She said she had a plan and wanted Mabel to help her, and not ask any questions, but get her skates and come out. Mabel did, and they went straight to George Morgan's house, which was only a few blocks away. He was very rich and had a beautiful house. An English butler came to the door. Mabel said she was so frightened her teeth chattered, but he smiled when he saw Kittie, and said yes, Mr. Morgan was home and at breakfast, and invited them in. When George came in he had a smoking-jacket on, and looked very pale and sad and romantic, Mabel thought, but he smiled, too, when he saw them, and shook hands and asked them if they had breakfasted.

Kittie said yes, but they had come to ask him to take them skating, and they were all ready and had brought their skates. His face fell, as real writers say, and he hesitated a little, but at last he said he'd go, and he excused himself, just as if they had been grown up, and went off to get ready.

When they were left alone a terrible doubt assailed Mabel, and she asked Kittie if she was going to ask George again to marry her. Kittie blushed and said she was not, of course, and that she knew better now. For it is indeed true that the human heart is not so easily turned from its dear object. We know that if once one truly loves it lasts forever and ever and ever, and then one dies and is buried with things the loved one wore.

Kittie said she had a plan to help George, and all Mabel had to do was to watch and keep on breathing. Mabel felt better then, and said she guessed she could do that. George came back all ready, and they started off. Kittie acted rather dark and mysterious, but Mabel conversed with George in the easy and pleasant fashion young men love. She told him all about school and how bad she was in mathematics; and he said he had been a duffer at it too, but that he had learned to shun it while there was yet time. And he advised her very earnestly to have nothing to do with it. Mabel didn't, either, after she came back to St. Catharine's;

and when Sister Irmingarde reproached her, Mabel said she was leaning on the judgment of a strong man, as woman should do. But Sister Irmingarde made her go on with the arithmetic just the same.

By and by they came to the river, and it was so early not

many people were skating there. When George had fastened on their skates—he did it in the nicest way, exactly as if they were grown up—Kittie looked more mysterious than ever, and she started off as fast as she could skate toward a little inlet where there was no one at all. George and Mabel followed her. George said he didn't know whether the ice was smooth in there, but Kittie kept right on, and George did not say any more. I guess he did not care much where he went. I suppose it disappoints a man when he wants to marry a woman and she won't. Now that I am beginning to study deeply this question of love, many things are clear to me.

Kittie kept far ahead, and all of a sudden Mabel saw that a little distance further on, and just ahead, there was a big black hole in the ice, and Kittie was skating straight toward it. Mabel tried to scream, but she says the sound froze on her pallid lips.

Then George saw the hole, too, and rushed toward Kittie, and quicker than I can write it Kittie went in that hole and down.

Mabel says George was there almost as soon, calling to Mabel to keep back out of danger. Usually when people have to rescue others, especially in stories, they call to some one to bring a board, and some one does, and it is easy. But very often in real life there isn't any board or any one to bring it, and this was indeed the desperate situation that confronted my hero. There was nothing to do but plunge in after Kittie, and he plunged, skates and all. Then Mabel heard him gasp and laugh a little, and he called out: “It’s all right, by Jove! The water isn’t much above my knees.” And even as he spoke Mabel saw Kittie rise in the water and sort of hurl herself at him and pull him down into the water, head and all. When they came up they were both half strangled, and Mabel was terribly frightened; for she thought George was mistaken about the depth, and they would both drown before her eyes; and then she would see that picture all her life, as they do in stories, and her hair would turn gray. She began to run up and down on the ice and scream; but even as she did so she heard these extraordinary words come from between Kittie James's chattering teeth:

"Now you are good and wet!"

George did not say a word. He confessed to Mabel afterwards that he thought poor Kittie had lost her mind through fear. But he tried the ice till he found a place that would hold him, and he got out and pulled Kittie out. As soon as Kittie was out she opened her mouth and uttered more remarkable words.

“Now,” she said, “I’ll skate till we get near the club-house. Then you must pick me up and carry me, and I’ll shut my eyes and let my head hang down.

And Mabel must cry—good and hard. Then you must send for Josephine and let her see how you've saved the life of her precious little sister."

Mabel said she was sure that Kittie was crazy, and next she thought George was crazy, too. For he bent and stared hard into Kittie's eyes for a minute, and then he began to laugh, and he laughed till he cried. He tried to speak, but he couldn't at first; and when he did the words came out between his shouts of boyish glee.

"Do you mean to say, you young monkey," he said, "that this is a put-up job?"

Kittie nodded as

solemnly as a fair young girl can nod when her clothes are dripping and her nose is blue with cold. When she did that, George roared again; then, as if he had remembered something, he caught her hands and began to skate very fast toward the club-house. He was a thoughtful young man, you see, and he wanted her to get warm. Perhaps he wanted to get warm, too. Anyhow, they started off, and as they went, Kittie opened still further the closed flower of her girlish heart. I heard that expression once, and I've always wanted to get it into one of my stories. I think this is a good place.

She told George she knew the hole in the ice, and that it wasn't deep; and she said she had done it all to make Josephine admire him and marry him.

"She will, too," she said. "Her dear little sister—the only one she's got." And Kittie went on to say what a terrible thing it would have been if she had died in the promise of her young life, till Mabel said she almost felt sure herself that George had saved her. But George hesitated. He said it wasn't "a square deal," whatever that means, but Kittie said no one need tell any lies. She had gone into the hole and George had pulled her out. She thought they needn't explain how deep it was, and George admitted thoughtfully that "no truly loving family should hunger for statistics at such a moment." Finally he said: "By Jove! I'll do it. All's fair in love and war." Then he asked Mabel if she thought she could "lend intelligent support to the star performers," and she said she could. So George picked Kittie up in his arms, and Mabel cried—she was so excited it was easy, and she wanted to do it all the time—and the sad little procession "homeward wended its weary way," as the poet says.

Mabel told me Kittie did her part like a real actress. She

shut her eyes and her head hung over George's arm, and her long, wet braid dripped as it trailed behind them. George laughed to himself every few minutes till they got near the club-house. Then he looked very sober, and Mabel Blossom knew her cue had come, the way it does to actresses, and she let out a wail that almost made Kittie sit up. It was 'most too much of a one, and Mr. Morgan advised her to "tone it down a little," because, he said, if she didn't they'd probably have Kittie buried before she could explain. But of course Mabel had not been prepared and had not had any practice. She muffled her sobs after that, and they sounded lots better. People began to rush from the club-house, and get blankets and whiskey, and telephone for doctors and for Kittie's family, and things got so exciting that nobody paid any attention to Mabel. All she had to do was to mop her eyes occasionally and keep a sharp lookout for Josephine; for of course, being an ardent student of life, like Maudie and me, she did not want to miss what came next.

Pretty soon a horse galloped up, all foaming at the mouth, and he was pulled back on his haunches, and Josephine and Mr. James jumped out of the buggy and rushed in, and there was more excitement. When George saw them coming he turned pale, Mabel said, and hurried off to change his clothes. One woman looked after him and said, “As modest as he is brave,” and cried over it. When Josephine and Mr. James came in there was more excitement, and Kittie opened one eye and shut it again right off, and the doctor said she was all right except for the shock, and her father and Josephine cried, so Mabel didn't have to any more. She was glad, too, I can tell you.

They put Kittie to bed in a room at the club, for the doctor said she was such a high-strung child it would be wise to keep her perfectly quiet for a few hours and take precautions against pneumonia. Then Josephine went around asking for Mr. Morgan.

By and by he came down, in dry clothes but looking dreadfully uncomfortable.

Mabel said she could imagine how he felt. Josephine was standing by the open fire when he entered the room, and no one else was there but Mabel. Josephine went right to him and put her arms around his neck.

“Dearest, dearest!” she said. “How can I ever thank you?” Her voice was very low, but Mabel heard it. George said right off, “There is a way.” That shows how quick and clever he is, for some men might not think of it. Then Mabel Blossom left the room, with slow, reluctant feet, and went up-stairs to Kittie.

That’s why Mabel has just gone to Kittie’s home for a few

days. She and Kittie are to be flower-maids at Josephine's wedding. I hope it is not necessary for me to explain to my intelligent readers that her husband will be George Morgan. Kittie says he confessed the whole thing to Josephine, and she forgave him, and said she would marry him anyhow; but she explained that she only did it on Kittie's account. She said she did not know to what lengths the child might go next.

So my young friends have gone to mingle in scenes of worldly gayety, and I sit here in the twilight looking at the evening star and writing about love. How true it is that the pen is mightier than the sword! Gayety is well in its place, but the soul of the artist finds its happiness in work and solitude. I hope Josephine will realize, though, why I cannot describe her wedding. Of course no artist of delicate sensibilities could describe a wedding when she hadn't been asked to it.

Poor Josephine! It seems very, very sad to me that she is marrying thus late in life and only on Kittie's account. Why, oh, why could she not have wed when she was young and love was in her heart!

THE END

ABOUT THE AUTHOR

Elizabeth Jordan was an American journalist, author, and suffragist. As the editor of Harper's Bazaar from 1900 to 1913, she helped start the careers of many great authors. Her heroine May Iverson was the star of many of her dozens of novels and short stories.

ABOUT THE COVER

The image on the cover is adapted from a photograph of an ivy covered wall at the University of Chicago by Quinn Dombrowski.

WHAT WE'RE ABOUT

I started making Super Large Print books for my grandma. I wanted books that she could keep reading as her glaucoma and macular degeneration advanced. So I chose a font originally designed for people with dyslexia, because the letters are bold and easy to distinguish. It is set at 30 pt, nearly twice the size of traditional Large Print books. Digital reading was too frustrating for my grandma. It could never offer the pleasures she had always associated with reading: the peacefulness of turning a page, the satisfaction in knowing a story has "this much left," and the comforting memories of adventure, companionship, and revelation she felt when seeing the cover of her favorite book. Part of what makes reading so relaxing and grounding is the tactile experience. I hope these books can bring joy to those who want to keep reading and to those who've never had the pleasure of curling up with a page turner.

Please let me know if these books are helpful to you and if you have any requests for new titles. To leave feedback and to see the complete and constantly updating catalog, please visit: superlargeprint.com

MORE BOOKS AT: superlargeprint.com

KEEP ON READING!

The cover is adapted from a photo by Quinn Dombrowski (CC BY-SA 2.0)
This book is set in a font designed by Abelardo Gonzalez called OpenDyslexic.

ISBN 9781095057780

Made in the USA
Middletown, DE
11 August 2020

15005476R00053